Puss in Boots

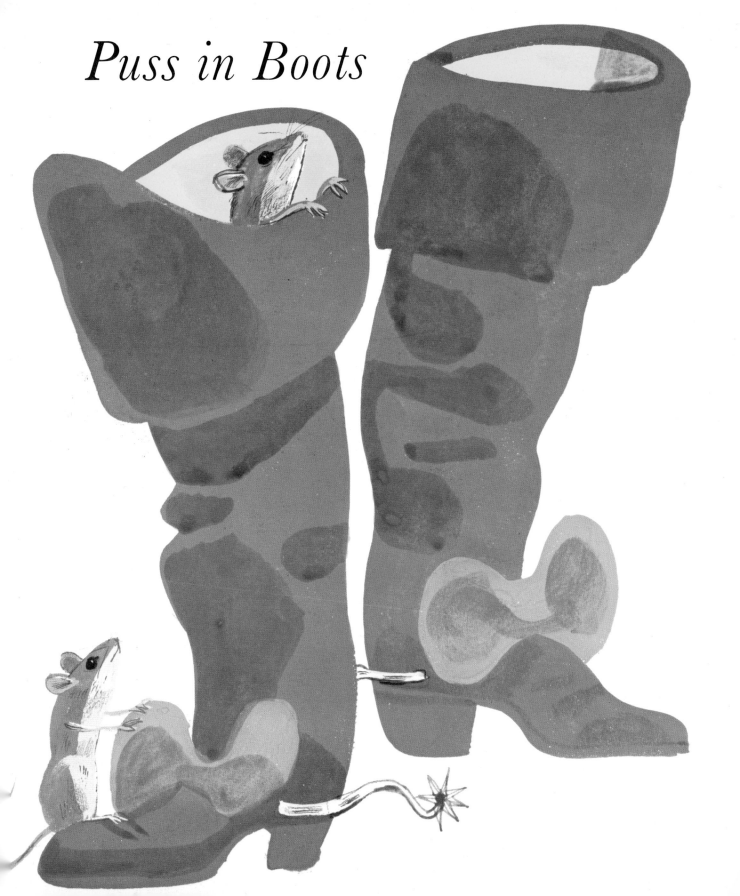

Puss in Boots

*Perrault's 'Maître Chat' retold and illustrated by
William Stobbs*

McGRAW-HILL BOOK COMPANY
New York   St. Louis   San Francisco

First published in 1975 by Kaye & Ward Ltd.
21 New Street, London EC2M 4NT.

Copyright © 1975 by Kaye & Ward Ltd.
First distribution in the United States of America
by McGraw-Hill, Inc., 1975.
Printed in Great Britain by
Reproduction by Colourcraftsmen Ltd., Chelmsford, Essex
Printed in Great Britain by Tindal Press, Chelmsford, Essex

Library of Congress Cataloging in Publication Data

Stobbs, William.
    Puss in Boots.

    SUMMARY: A cat wins his master a fortune and the
hand of a princess.
    [1. Fairy tales. 2. Folklore—France]
I. Perrault, Charles, 1628-1703. Le chat botté.
II. Title.
PZ8.S68Pu3   398.2′452′974428   [E]   74-25152
ISBN 0-07-061582-9
ISBN 0-07-061581-0 lib. bdg.

There was once a miller who had three sons.
When the miller died, he left them his windmill, his
donkey and his cat. The eldest son had the windmill,
the second the donkey and the youngest got the cat.

The youngest son was very sad: "With the
windmill and the donkey, my brothers will have
no trouble in making a living. But I will starve
to death."

The cat heard this, and, looking very grave and
serious, said:

"Master, give me a sack, and have a pair of boots made for me, and you will see what I can do for you."

His master could not believe this, but he knew the cat was clever at catching rats and mice, so he began to cheer up.

When the cat had got what he had asked for, he pulled on his boots and set off, with the sack over his shoulder.

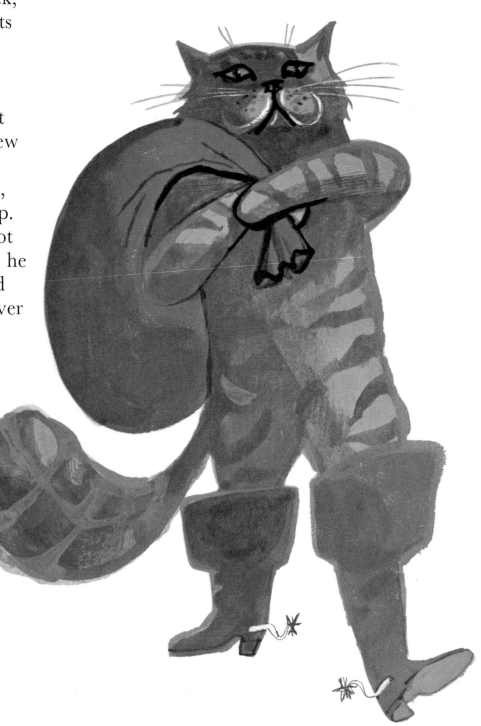

When he came to a cornfield, the cat hid himself among the corn, but kept his sack open, and when two partridges went into his sack, he pulled tight the strings and caught them both. Then he set off to see the King.

When the cat arrived at the palace and was taken to the King, he made a deep bow and said: "Your Majesty, the Marquis of Carrabas begs you to accept this present."

The King was very pleased with the partridges.

The cat continued to bring the King gifts of game for the next two or three months. Then one day, when the cat knew that the King was going for a drive along the riverbank with his daughter, the most beautiful princess in the world, the cat said to his master: "Do as I tell you and your fortune is made. Just bathe in the river at the place I show you, and leave the rest to me."

The miller's son did as he was told. When
the King's carriage came by, the cat cried out,
"Help! Help! The Marquis of Carrabas is drowning!"
The King put his head out of the carriage window and,
recognizing the cat, sent his footmen to rescue the Marquis.
Then the cat told the King that thieves had stolen his master's
clothes. The truth was that the cat had himself hidden
them under a big stone. As soon as the King
heard this, he ordered his footmen to fetch
one of his best suits for the Marquis to wear.

The Marquis looked very handsome
in his borrowed clothes, and the princess
fell madly in love with him.

The King then asked the Marquis to
join them, and the carriage continued
on its way.

The cat, very pleased to see his plan already beginning to work, ran ahead. Meeting some men mowing a meadow, he said to them: "If you do not tell the King that these meadows belong to the Marquis of Carrabas, you will be chopped up into pieces as small as mincemeat."

And when the carriage passed by a moment later, and the King stopped to ask who owned the meadows, the men said, "The Marquis of Carrabas," for they were frightened by the cat's threats.

Then the cat, still running on ahead, met some harvesters. The cat said: "If you do not tell the King that these cornfields belong to the Marquis of Carrabas, you will be chopped up into pieces as small as mincemeat." And again, when the King came by a moment later and wanted to know who owned the cornfields, he received the same reply.

At last, the cat came to a beautiful castle surrounded by a deep moat. The castle belonged to a very rich Ogre, who was the real owner of the fields the cat had claimed for his master.

Boldly, the cat walked in and asked to speak to him.

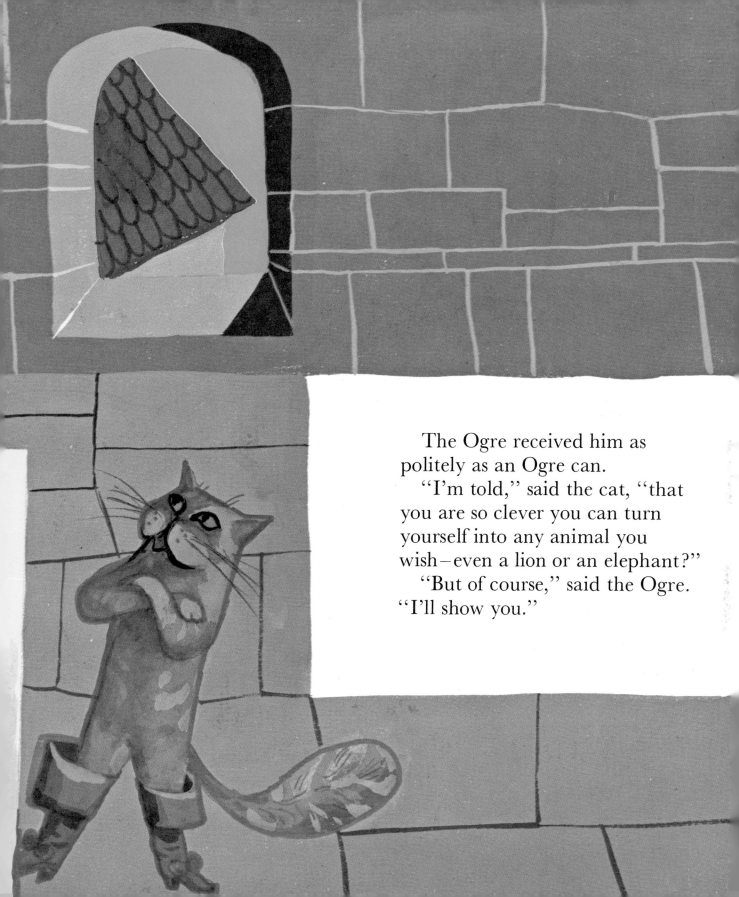

The Ogre received him as politely as an Ogre can.

"I'm told," said the cat, "that you are so clever you can turn yourself into any animal you wish—even a lion or an elephant?"

"But of course," said the Ogre. "I'll show you."

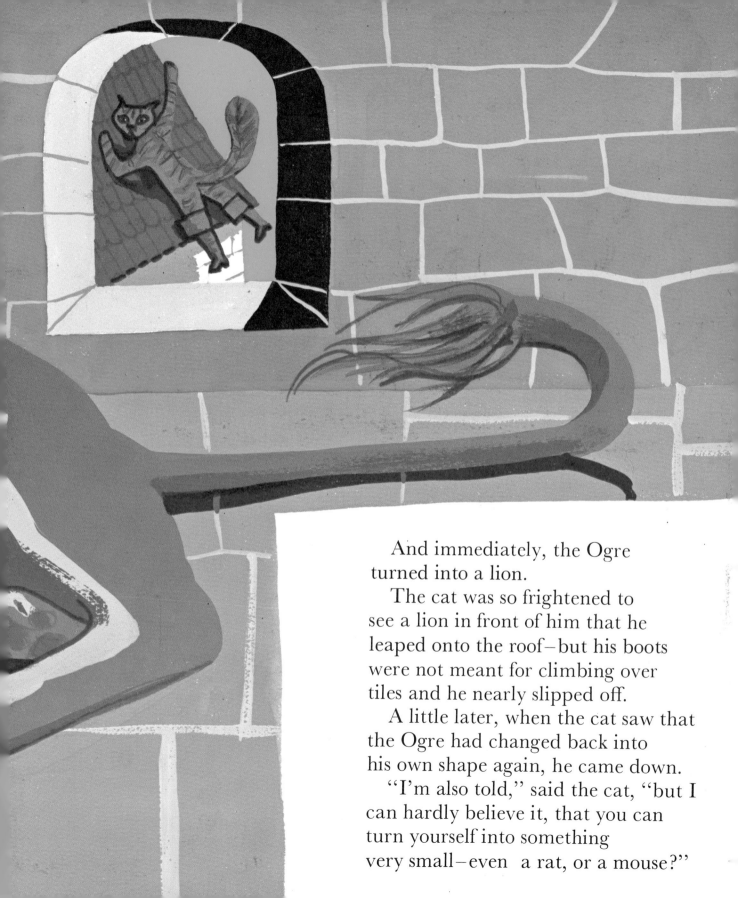

And immediately, the Ogre
turned into a lion.

The cat was so frightened to
see a lion in front of him that he
leaped onto the roof—but his boots
were not meant for climbing over
tiles and he nearly slipped off.

A little later, when the cat saw that
the Ogre had changed back into
his own shape again, he came down.

"I'm also told," said the cat, "but I
can hardly believe it, that you can
turn yourself into something
very small—even a rat, or a mouse?"

"Nothing could be easier," said the
Ogre. He then turned himself into a mouse
and began to scamper across the floor.
The cat pounced on the mouse and ate it up.

Meanwhile, the King's carriage was passing the castle. The King thought it was such a beautiful castle he must see inside. As soon as the cat heard the noise of the carriage passing over the draw-bridge, he ran outside to meet it.

"Welcome to the castle of the Marquis of Carrabas, Your Majesty," said the cat.

"What?" cried the King. "Is this castle yours also, Marquis? May we go inside?"

Then the King, and the Marquis with the young princess on his arm, followed the cat into the castle.

They found themselves in a great hall
with a marvelous feast spread out before
them.

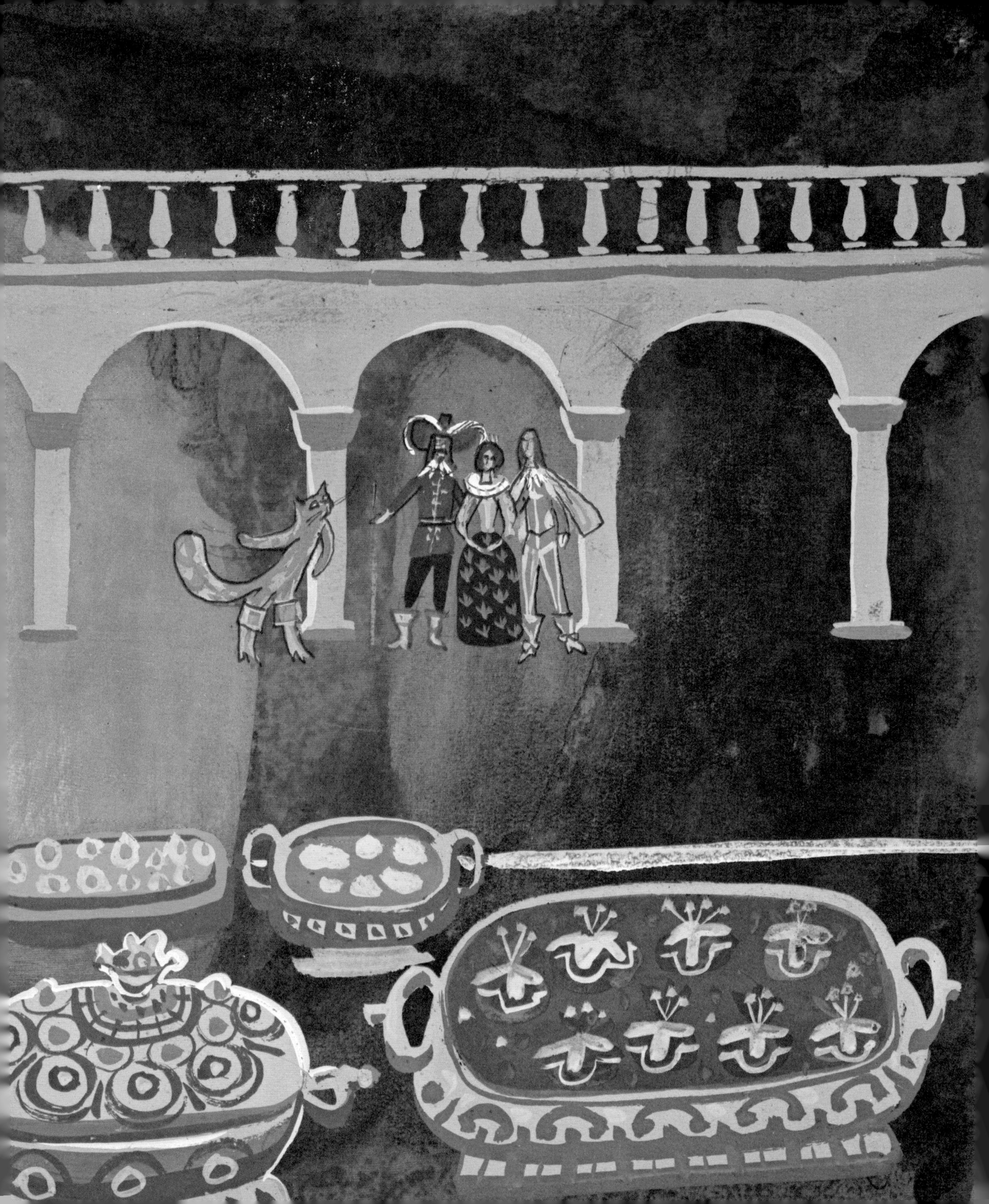

After the King had drunk five or six glasses of wine, he said: "Would you do me the honor of marrying my daughter?"

The Marquis made a very deep bow and accepted, and he married the princess that very day.

As for the cat, he was made a great
Lord and no longer chased mice, except
to amuse himself.